ZIZU
Loses His Stripes

For Saerah
(Mum)

Written by: Peter Barron
Illustrated by: Jonathan Raiseborough

"It's hot today," sighed Zizu,
"I think I'll have a swim."
The water looked so cool,
The zebra jumped right in.

"Now I'm wet," thought Zizu,
"I'll roll around in mud."
The mud was nice and gooey,
What fun - it felt so good!

But when he looked into the pool,
Every inch of him was black.
He'd lost his lovely stripey coat,

a **HORSE**
was staring
back!

"Excuse me, have you seen my stripes?"
He asked Geoffrey the giraffe.
"No, I'm sorry, little Zizu,"
Replied Geoffrey with a laugh.

"*I'll help you search,*" said Geoffrey,
With his long neck in the air.
He looked on every treetop,
But Zizu's stripes weren't there.

Along came Cody crocodile,
Who searched the riverbed.
But when he popped back up again,
Cody shook his head.

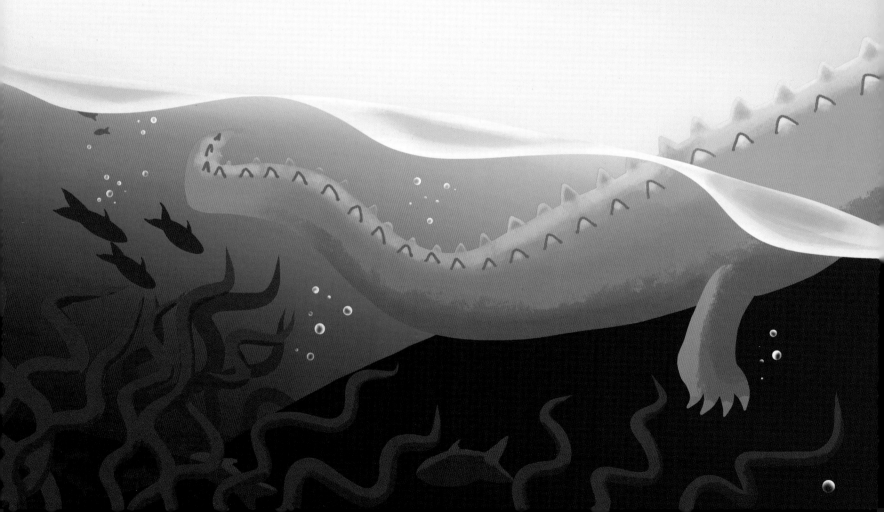

Priscilla gorilla thumped her chest,

And swung from tree to tree.

But she couldn't find the stripes,

So she went home for her tea.

Poppy parrot stretched her wings,
And soared into the sky.
She checked behind the moon and stars,
And clouds that floated by.

Just then a trumpet sounded,
And guess who came along?

Ellie's always helpful,
Whenever something's wrong.

"Zizu's lost his stripes,"
they cried,
"They're nowhere to be seen."

Ellie smiled then dunked her trunk,
Into a nearby stream.

She sucked in lots of water,
It seemed to take an hour.
Then she aimed at Zizu zebra,
And gave her friend a shower!

"They're back! They're back!"
beamed Zizu.
"Oh, goodness, golly gosh!

"I didn't lose my stripes at all,
"What I needed was a wash!"

So Zizu went home happy,
That's where the story ends.
Let's always do the best we can,
To be kind to all our friends.

THE END

ZIZU AND HIS FRIENDS

Zizu Zebra

Zizu is playful and very lovable but he can be a little bit nervous and shy, so he needs lots of support from his friends.

Geoffrey Giraffe

Geoffrey is very calm and wise. That's because he's very tall and can see everything that's happening in the jungle.

Cody Crocodile

Cody can sometimes be a bit snappy when he gets hungry, but he's learning to be kind - especially if any of his friends can't swim.

Priscilla Gorilla

Priscilla doesn't know her own strength, and can sometimes be a bit clumsy, but she's loyal and protects her friends whenever they need her.

Poppy Parrot

Poppy can be very noisy with all her squawking but she's learned to be quiet when someone else is talking.

Ellie Elephant

Ellie is the most helpful elephant in the world. She's very clever and always knows what to do when something goes wrong.

There are lots more friends and you'll meet them soon in other Zizu books

ZIZU SAYS...

"We're all different – that's what makes us special."

"Friends should always help each other."

"Never be afraid to ask for help."

"Help others if they look sad, scared or lonely."

ZIZU'S CHALLENGE:

Can you count all the snakes in this book?

Answer: 6

FOUNDATION

A contribution from every book sold will be donated to The Zizus Foundation, which is dedicated to helping fund early-years education for children who might otherwise miss out. To find out more go to:

www.zizusfoundation.com

This book is supported by the North East Autism Society